bunny slopes

Claudia Rueda

chronicle books·san francisco

Hello?

Oh, it's you.
Want to join me for a ski day?

But where's all the snow?

Maybe we can **make** some!
Could you please

((shake))

the book?

That's better.
But could you

shake

the book much harder?

Um, that might have been
a little **too** much.

Can you tap tap tap
the top of the book? That should
pack down the snow.

Perfect. Thank you!

Now maybe you can help me
go downhill. Could you

tilt

the book to your right?

That's not exactly **down**hill . . .
maybe you could

the book a bit more?

Carrots!
What fun. Thank you.

Yikes!

Quick! 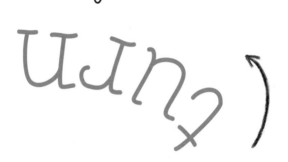 the book.

→

Then flip the page.

Umph.

Okay, would you *turn*

the book
right-side up?

Then flip the page.

→

Thanks!
Really, I'm fine.

Let's try that cliff again.
Would you

tilt

the book to your right?
I'll need some speed!

Perfect!
Get ready . . .

...to jump!

Zowie!
Easy as carrot cake.

A hole? No problem.

Ha! I told you.

Aaaagh!

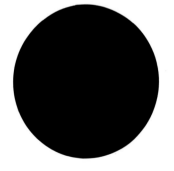

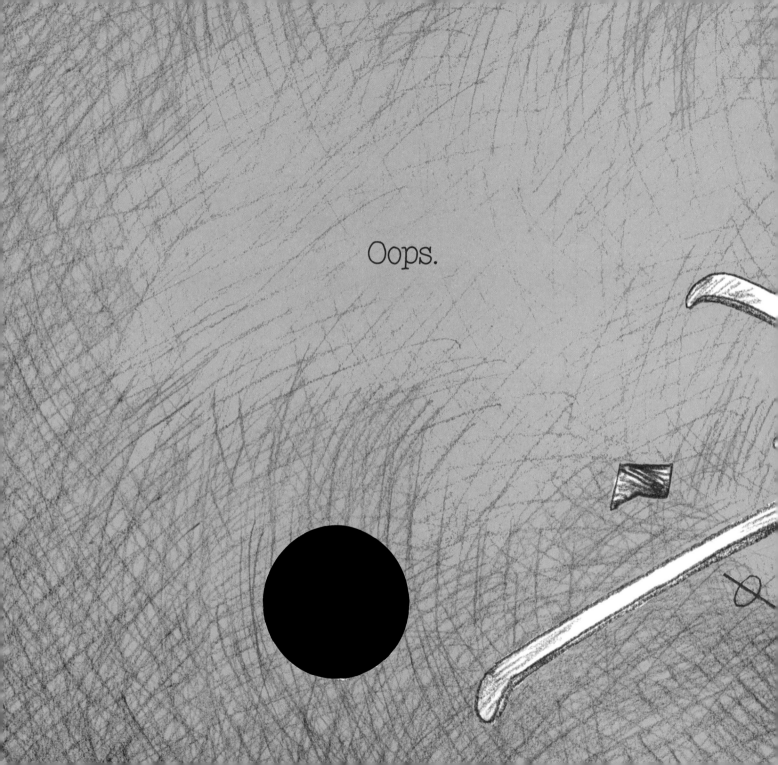

Oh. Hi, Mom!

Time to warm up after
a long day on the slopes.

This one is for you.

Bunny would like to dedicate this book
to **you**, for all your help on the slopes today.

Also dedicated to Cata and Cami.
—Claudia

Library of Congress Cataloging-in-Publication Data available.
ISBN 978-1-4521-4197-8

Manufactured in China.

Design by Amelia Mack.
Typeset in Sprout.
The illustrations in this book were rendered in charcoal and digitally.

10 9 8 7 6 5 4 3 2 1

Chronicle Books LLC
680 Second Street
San Francisco, California 94107
www.chroniclekids.com